TRACTOR MAC

TRACTOR MAC
ARRIVES AT THE FARM

Written and illustrated by
BILLY STEERS

FARRAR STRAUS GIROUX • **NEW YORK**

SIBLEY THE HORSE LIVED on Stony
Meadow Farm. He was a hard worker.
Tug and pull, haul and drag. He did
the work of two strong horses.

Sibley's days were spent plowing in the spring,

mowing in the summer,

harvesting in the fall,

and logging in the winter.

Sibley's favorite job was pulling the hay wagon at the summer picnics.

The children would all cheer for Sibley and give him treats of apples and carrots.

One day, the animals heard a strange noise.
Chug! Chugga! Pop!

They looked out of the barn.

A large red machine was parked in the farmyard spewing smoke. Farmer Bill was seated on a bright shiny new tractor. He had a big smile on his face.

That evening, Farmer Bill moved the tractor into the
barn. The animals came over to greet the newcomer.

"What big black rubber tires you have," said Carla the chicken.

"Look at all of your wires, gears, and cables!" exclaimed Pete the pig.

"Welcome to Stony Meadow Farm," said Sam the ram.

"Welcome! Welcome!" the others all cried.

The red tractor smiled. "Howdy-do!" he said. "My name is Mac. I can do the work of ten horses, and I'm happy to be here."

The animals gasped.

"Ten horses!"

"You must be *really* strong!"

That night, Sibley was not able to sleep. Visions of mechanical horses danced in his head. Could Mac really do the work of ten horses? What would be left for Sibley to do?

Early the next morning, Farmer Bill climbed into Mac's seat and started the engine. Mac rumbled to life, and they headed for the fields. Sibley waited to be tacked up for the day's work, but nobody came.

All that day, Sibley listened to the other animals' chatter.

"Did you see how fast Mac plowed the fields?" clucked the chickens.

"He delivered the hay in less than an hour," baaed the sheep.

"He hauled all the wood for the new roof," squealed the pigs.

As the days passed, it was clear that Mac had taken over all of Sibley's jobs.

"Soon they'll be turning you out to pasture," said Margot the cow. "You'll probably never have to work another day in your life."

Just then, Sibley heard the sound of children. Maybe they were coming to the barnyard for a hayride. He galloped out of the barn . . .

. . . and stopped abruptly at the fence. There was Mac, pulling a dozen cheering children in a hay wagon. Sibley's hay wagon!

Sibley had never felt so sad and useless in his whole life.

What good is a workhorse who cannot work?

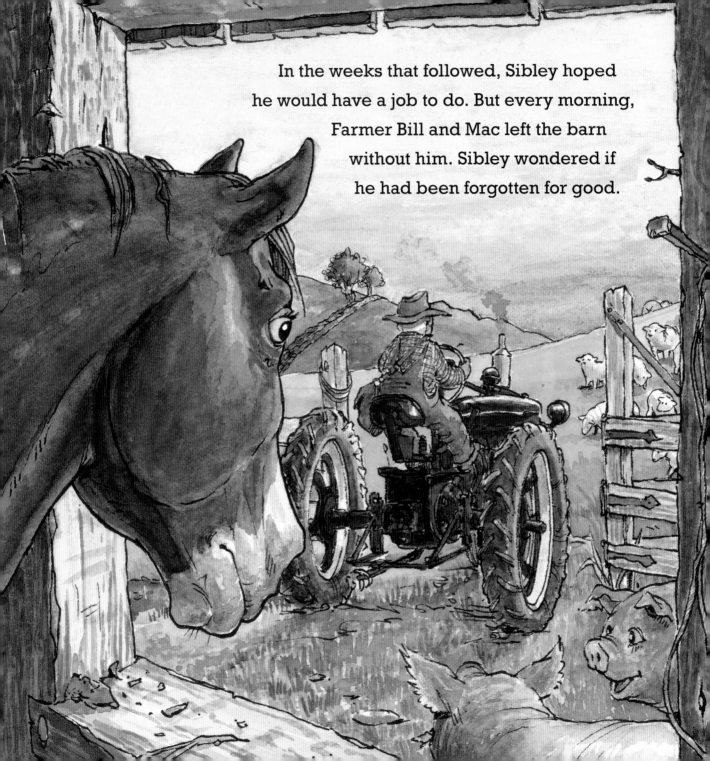

In the weeks that followed, Sibley hoped he would have a job to do. But every morning, Farmer Bill and Mac left the barn without him. Sibley wondered if he had been forgotten for good.

Finally, one day Farmer Bill came back to the farm without Mac. "Sibley, old lad, I need your help. We have a problem that only you can fix."

Rain had fallen during the night. The farmer led Sibley through the soggy grass to a far field where the ground was soaked with water.

There sat Mac, up to his axles in mud.

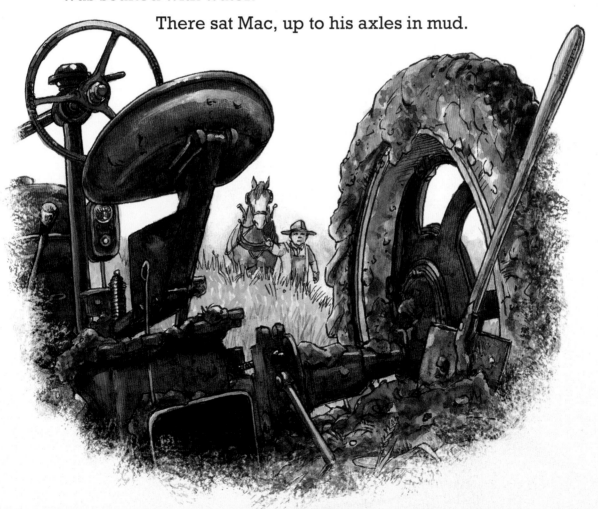

With a tug and a yank, Sibley wrenched Mac free from the mud.

Then he spent the rest of the day working in the soggy field while Mac sat behind the stone wall.

When it was time to go back to the barn, Mac said, "Thanks for rescuing me, Sibley."

Farmer Bill patted Sibley on the neck. "You were a big help today," he said.

From that day on, Farmer Bill let both
Sibley and Mac work side by side.
They became the best of friends.